Henry Augustus Pilsbry

Sea Shells of the Jersey Shore

Henry Augustus Pilsbry

Sea Shells of the Jersey Shore

ISBN/EAN: 9783337391904

Printed in Europe, USA, Canada, Australia, Japan

Cover: Foto ©Andreas Hilbeck / pixelio.de

More available books at **www.hansebooks.com**

OF THE

JERSEY SHORE,

BY

H. A. PILSBRY,

CONSERVATOR OF THE CONCHOLOGICAL SECTION OF THE
ACADEMY OF NATURAL SCIENCES OF PHILADELPHIA.

ASBURY PARK NOVELTY CO.,
ASBURY PARK, NEW JERSEY,
1891.

PREFACE.

Among the thousands who visit the New Jersey coast during the summer months, there are no doubt many who would take pleasure in becoming better acquainted with the sea shore and its many forms of life.

The desire of the author to assist in such an introduction to nature, has resulted in this little book.

In the following pages all the commoner shells of our shore are illustrated and described; there may be other interesting species found. In that case the author will gladly name them if sent to him, and include them in future editions.

The illustrations are partly original, but they are mainly photographic reproductions of those of Gould's "Invertebrata of Massachusetts."

H. A. P.

Philadelphia, *June*, 1891

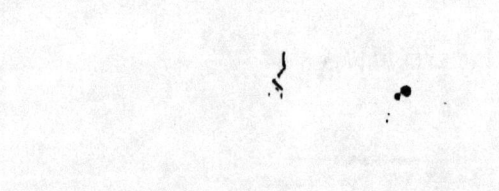

SHELLS OF THE JERSEY SHORE.

CHAPTER I.—Beginnings.

A walk along the beach is the best beginning in the collection and love of shells. Not the most brilliant shells that can be bought give us the pleasure we have in those of our own collecting; the additional joy of *discovery* belongs to these.

We will take a few of the shells we find in our first walk, and see what they will tell us. A common " round clam" is almost certain to be one of them. The outside is a dingy brownish; within it is white with a purple spot, and various lines and markings.

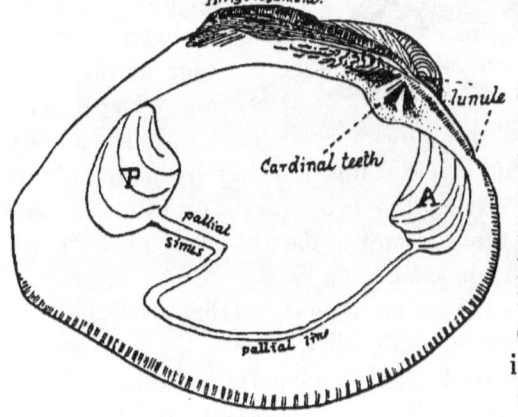

It is as if in a stroll on the Campagna we were to find an old Roman coin or medal. How much the pleasure of finding would be increased by our being able to decipher its Latin legend; so it is with our

Fig. 1. Inside view of Venus mercenaria, the round clam.

common clam shell; each of its lines has a meaning which we may learn to read. 7

First, we see that the shell is composed of two parts, called *valves*, fastened together at the back by a strong but flexible ligament. Below this, the hinge has several prominences, called "*teeth*" which fit into corresponding cavities in the opposite valve. These strengthen the hinge and make it open and close accurately. Above the hinge, projects the "beak" or *umbo* of the valve. At each end of the shell there is a scar (A, P) marking the places where two muscles are attached. These muscles are called "adductors" because they close the shell. The line connecting the scars of the adductors is where the *mantle* or lining of the shell is attached,

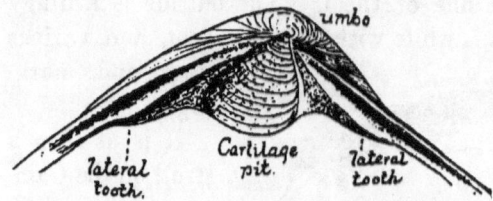

and is called the *pallial line*. The edge of the mantle extends to the edge of the shell, and gradually builds the latter

Fig. 2. Hinge of Beach clam, Mactra solidissima.

up by depositing thin layers of lime. A bay (or *pallial sinus*) in this line indicates that the two siphons or tubes through which the animal draws water to the gills, and expels it, are long, as in the common sand clam.

In some bivalves there is no ligament on the outside, it being transformed into a cushion of cartilage which occupies a pit or cavity below the beaks. Such a one is *Mactra* (Fig. 2.)

Univalves, or spiral shells, called GASTEROPODS in scientific language, have the shell in one piece, usually in the form of a spiral cone. The opening or *aperture* is generally round or oval, and has either a continuous even margin, or a notch

SHELLS OF THE JERSEY SHORE.

CHAPTER I.—BEGINNINGS.

A walk along the beach is the best beginning in the collection and love of shells. Not the most brilliant shells that can be bought give us the pleasure we have in those of our own collecting; the additional joy of *discovery* belongs to these.

We will take a few of the shells we find in our first walk, and see what they will tell us. A common "round clam" is almost certain to be one of them. The outside is a dingy brownish; within it is white with a purple spot, and various lines and markings.

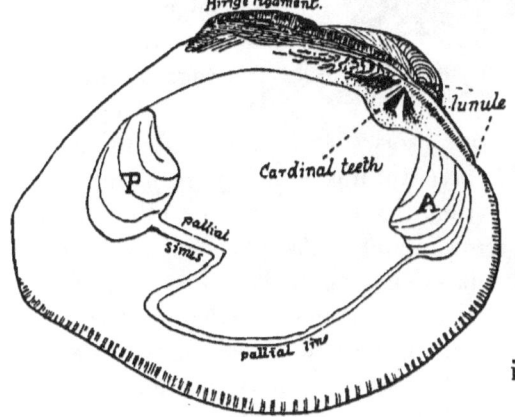

Fig. 1. Inside view of Venus mercenaria, the round clam.

It is as if in a stroll on the Campagna we were to find an old Roman coin or medal. How much the pleasure of finding would be increased by our being able to decipher its Latin legend; so it is with our common clam shell; each of its lines has a meaning which we may learn to read.

7

First, we see that the shell is composed of two parts, called *valves*, fastened together at the back by a strong but flexible ligament. Below this, the hinge has several prominences, called "*teeth*" which fit into corresponding cavities in the opposite valve. These strengthen the hinge and make it open and close accurately. Above the hinge, projects the "beak" or *umbo* of the valve. At each end of the shell there is a scar (A, P) marking the places where two muscles are attached. These muscles are called "adductors" because they close the shell. The line connecting the scars of the adductors is where the *mantle* or lining of the shell is attached, and is called the *pallial line*. The edge of the mantle extends to the edge of the shell, and gradually builds the latter

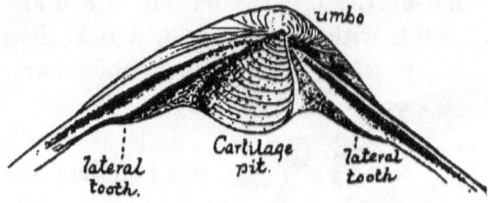

Fig. 2. Hinge of Beach clam, Mactra solidissima.

up by depositing thin layers of lime. A bay (or *pallial sinus*) in this line indicates that the two siphons or tubes through which the animal draws water to the gills, and expels it, are long, as in the common sand clam.

In some bivalves there is no ligament on the outside, it being transformed into a cushion of cartilage which occupies a pit or cavity below the beaks. Such a one is *Mactra* (Fig. 2.)

Univalves, or spiral shells, called GASTEROPODS in scientific language, have the shell in one piece, usually in the form of a spiral cone. The opening or *aperture* is generally round or oval, and has either a continuous even margin, or a notch or canal at its lower part. The axis around which it is coiled is called the *columella* (little column) and is only visible at the aperture, unless the shell be broken. The *suture* is the line where the *whorls* or turns of the shell come together. The names of these parts are marked on figure 3.

* * *

The shell is a part of the animal, just as the bones are a part of the human body ; and while life lasts, the soft part of the mollusk is never separated from its shell.

Fig. 3. A gasteropod shell, Eupleura caudata.

The names of shells are derived from Greek or Latin words, because these languages are studied in all countries, and so the confusion of having as many different names for each species as there are modern languages is avoided. Each mollusk has two names : that of the *species* or particular kind, which is written last (corresponding to the "Christian name" of a person), and that of the *genus* or group, which is written first. The generic name is a noun ; the specific name an adjective or genitive form of a proper noun. The first name should be written with a capital, the second with a small letter unless it is derived from a proper name. After the name, is written the initials or name of the naturalist who first described and named the species. English pronunciation may be used for scientific names unless the Roman is preferred. The accented syllable is indicated in the text.

The most merciful way to kill living mollusks is to place them in a basin and pour water nearly boiling hot, over them. They die almost instantly, and may be removed with a knife or pin. If quite small, they need not be removed from the shell. The *operculum* or plate which closes the aperture of Gastropod shells, should be kept with the shell. Bivalves should be tied together until dry, so that the valves will not be broken apart.

CHAPTER II.—OYSTERS AND SCALLOPS.

We will begin with the most simply organized class of mollusks, those having bivalve shells. The animal has broad gills on each side of the body, to which water is brought by a tube. The food consisting of minute creatures is also strained out of this water. They have a fleshy "foot" used for digging, but no head or eyes.

The oysters and scallops differ from other bivalve shells in having only one muscle for pulling the valves together. The place where the muscle is attached to the shell is at about the middle of each valve. They lie upon one side, instead of standing upon the end or edge, as other bivalves do, and the under valve becomes flattened in consequence. They move about so little when a residence has once been selected, that the "foot" is all but lost from sheer want of exercise.

The first of this tribe (at least on bills-of-fare) is the Oyster **Ostræa virginica** Gmelin, a bivalve of such broad repute as to need no introduction to us ; for *Ostræa* has been talked of, written about and eaten since before the founding of Rome.

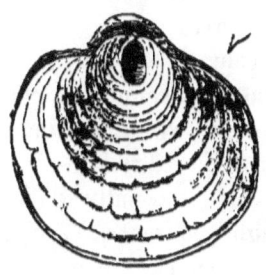

Our oysters build a rough, rude, irregular shell, and the muscle-scar or "eye" is of a dark purple color.

Next to the Oysters come those pretty little scale-like golden and silver shells which dot the sands,

Fig. 4. Anomia simplex.

Anomia simplex Orb. "*Anomia*" means *nameless ;* but they have several names for all that; "Saddle-oysters" is one of

11

them. The shell is thin and yellow, of a tough, fibrous texture, not nearly so fragile as it looks. They attach themselves in early life to a shell or rock, by the solid "plug" extending through a round hole in the lower or flat valve. The other valve is quite convex, and is the one usually found on the beach. You must find living ones to get both valves together. When *Anomia* grows on a scallop shell its own shell becomes fluted in harmony with the scallop. Headless, footless and blind; but still like everything *living*, they reflect in themselves the beauty or rudeness of their surroundings.

The Scallops or Pectens differ from the other bivalves having

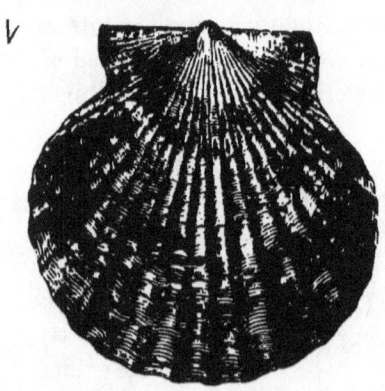

ing a single muscle, in being much more symmetrical or regular in the growth of the shell. The two valves are almost equally convex.

Our common species, **Pecten irradians** Linné, is a circular shell, fluted, having about eighteen rounded ribs on each valve. It is usually dark, with light concentric zones, but the young are quite prettily marked with zigzag

Fig. 5. Pecten irradians.

stripes. They prefer a sandy bottom and shallow water, and may be found scattered far and wide all along our shores. Pectens are capital eating; and thousands of bushels are sent to the markets of the New England cities and of New York; but in the restaurants of Philadelphia, one usually asks for them in vain. The central muscle only is eaten, and it makes a delicious fry. Other modes of cooking I cannot commend so highly.

CHAPTER III.—MUSSELS.

The mussels are oblong shells with two equal valves, covered

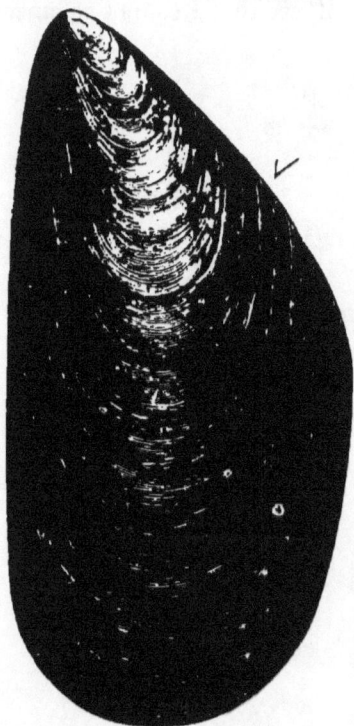

Fig. 6.   Mytilus edulis.

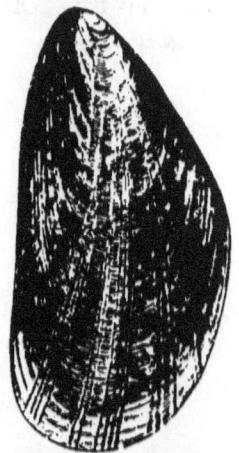

Fig. 7.   Mytilus edulis, var. pellucidus.

with an epidermis, and having two adductor muscles.   In the true mussels or *Mytilidæ* the adductor muscle nearest to the beaks is very small, and the hinge practically without teeth.   They live attached to wooden piles or anything convenient, by a cord composed of strong threads.   This cord is called the " byssus."

The common mussel, **Mytilus edulis** Linné, (figs. 6, 7) is smooth, varying in color from black to light yellow. The lighter specimens frequently have radiating green lines and stripes and are very beautiful. Mussels are considered edible, but I would not recommend them to anyone but book-reviewers and other natural enemies of mankind.

Closely related to these are the Horse mussels, **Modiola plica-tula** Lam. They have the beaks a little distance from the narrow end of the shell, not at the end as *Mytilus* has. The larger end of the shell is finely fluted, as well as a little triangle at the smaller end. They are found living where there is an admixture of fresh water.

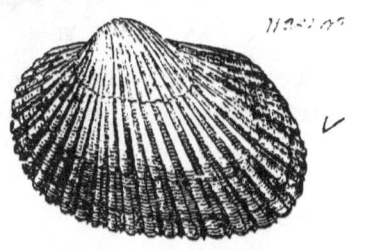

Fig. 9. Arca transversa.

Fig. 8. Modiola plicatula.

The Ark Mussel family or *Arcidæ* have the beaks near the middle of the hinge line, the two adductor muscles equal, the hinge furnished with many very fine interlocking teeth, like fine comb teeth. The outside is fluted like a cockle. They have red blood, an exception to the rule that the blood of mollusks is colorless. From this peculiarity Arca is sometimes called the "bloody clam."

An *Arca* not often found in good condition on our coast is **Arca transversa** Say, (Fig. 9). This is an oblong shell, sculptured with about twenty-five squarish riblets. The brown epidermis is generally lacking on specimens washed up on the beach.

Fig. 10. Arca pexata.

Another species often found all along the Jersey coast is **Arca pexata** Say. It is more rounded than the other species, and the comb-toothed hinge-line is more curved. It has about thirty-two radiating riblets, and when fresh is covered with a dark epidermis which is hairy in the grooves between the ribs.

CHAPTER IV.—CLAMS.

One of the commonest clams all up and down the coast is the Round Clam or Quahog, **Venus mercenaria** Linné, a large, solid, oval shell, dull enough outside, although the young are occasionally marked with zigzag stripes. It is white inside, with a spot of purple at one or both ends. Everybody knows that our red skinned predecessors used to carve their currency or "wampum" from these shells. Quahogs are eaten everywhere, but they are not nearly so tender and delicate as the "Little Neck" or "Sand" clams (*Mya arenaria*).

Fig. 11. Venus mercenaria. One-half natural size.

Fig. 12. Cytherea convexa.

17

The Little Round Clam, **Cytherea convexa** Say, is much like the *Venus;* but it is more rounded, instead of triangular-oval; very convex. Inside it is pure white. It is not a common shell.

The shell here pictured is a most familiar object on the

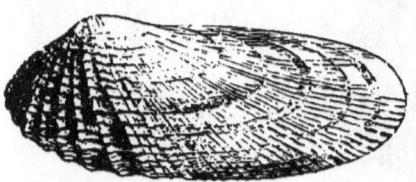

sands. It is the **Petricola pholad i f o r m i s** Lam. " False Pholas" would be a good common name, if it needs one, for it is very much like a *Pholas* in

Fig. 13.   Petricola pholadiformis.

form and ornamentation of the surface. Not content with aping the Pholas' person, this Petricola goes so far as to copy their manner of living too. It bores into hard mud, or sometimes into wood softened by lying in sea water.

Now comes one of the smallest and prettiest of the common clams, **Donax fossor** Say. When you find Donax at all, you are likely to find about a million of them. The shell is triangular-oblong, smooth except for faint radiating riblets, and of

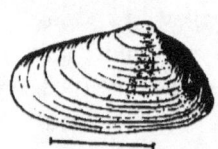

a pure white or yellowish color, generally having a faint purplish streak from the beaks downward. The inside is white, tinted with faint orange, or is of a royal purple color. The edge of the valve is finely crenulated. When you find living

Fig. 14.   Donax fossor.

Donax take a few home in a bottle of sea water. They will soon reach out the long slender siphons, one for drawing the water in, the other conducting it out, after the food particles are strained from it and the gills have absorbed its oxygen. From the other end of the shell the white muscular foot is seen protruding.

Another little shell having the form of Donax, is **Tellina** ✓

tenera Say. It is much more fragile than Donax, wider, and the edges of the valves are smooth, not crenulated. The color is generally a delicate pink

Fig. 15.
Tellina tenera. or deep rose color.

Macoma baltica Linné, another member of the *Tellinidœ* or Tellen family, is larger than the last, and rounder in outline. It is either white or pink, and is covered with a very

thin brown epidermis, usually worn off except around the lower edge.

Macoma tenta Say is longer and narrower than *T. tenera* and white or yellowish. These tiny species are our

Fig. 16.   Macoma baltica. northern representatives of the family to which that beautiful white, pink-rayed, *Tellina radiata* of Florida belongs.

The Soft Clam or Sand Clam, **Mya arenaria** Linn. is by far the choicest of our food clams ; but all its tenderness and

sweetness are concealed beneath a rude and unpolished exterior, as the novelists say. Mya belongs to that class of bivalves which have the lig-

Fig. 17.
Macoma tenta. ament for opening the shell *inside* or below the hinge-line, instead of outside—an important difference from a mechanical point of view, for in pulling the valves shut, the ligament or cartilage is *compressed* in these forms, whilst in those with an external ligament, such as Venus, Solen, Tellina,

etc., it is *stretched*. In Mya there is an erect, spoon-shaped process in one valve, for the attachment of this cartilage, and

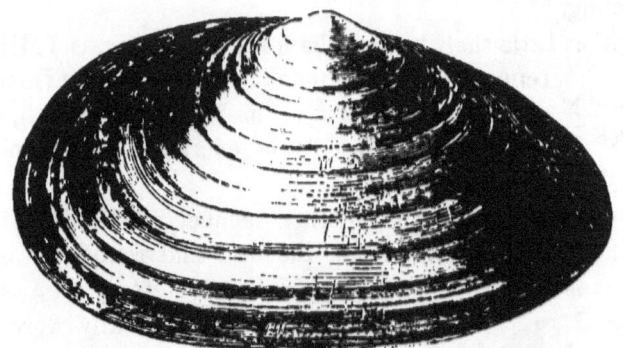

Fig. 18. Mya arenaria.

a triangular pit in the other valve. The valves gape at each end of the shell; the siphons of the animal are very long.

Fig. 19. Mactra solidissima.

The Beach Clam family, *Mactridæ*, have the cartilage pit of the same form in both valves, and on each side of it there are narrow lateral teeth ; the valves shut closely all around.

The Beach Clam, **Mactra solidissima** Chemnitz, is a smooth, yellowish-white shell. It grows to a very large size, and is so abundant that one cannot walk the beach without seeing quantities of them.

Frequently they are found with a very neatly bevelled round hole near the beaks. This is the work of the *Natica*, a fat and good-natured looking mollusk, but secretly most blood-thirsty. Boring along through the sand, like a mole, goes the Natica until he finds a clam ; he then brings his tongue, armed with rows of sharp teeth, into play, and bores a hole through the shell of his victim, through which the soft tissues may be eaten at leisure. This is a very ingenious way for Natica to get a meal, but the feelings of the clam at being bored to death are not pleasant to think about ; but it is the way of the world.

> " Big fleas have little fleas
> And smaller fleas to bite 'em ;
> And these again have other fleas,
> And so *ad infinitum.*"

A little brother of the big fellow last pictured is the Little Beach Clam, **Mactra lateralis** Say. The shell is small, thin and differs from young of the larger species in having a rather sharp and distinct ridge running from the beaks downward and backward ; in being more triangular and less compressed. It has also less of a yellow tint than *M. sol-*

Fig. 20. Mactra lateralis.

idissima.

The Smooth Cockle, **Cardium mortoni** Conrad, is rather rare on the New Jersey coast, but common southward. Cardium differs from most of the preceding clams in having lat-

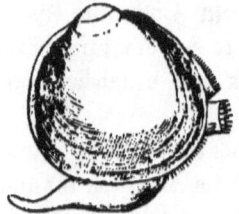

Fig. 21. Cardium mortoni.

teral teeth on each side of the cardinal teeth, which are right under the beaks. The shell is rather globular, rather thin, smooth and white outside, tinted with yellow inside, with a reddish-brown stripe or blotch on the posterior end. By holding a valve up to a strong light, delicate riblets may be seen through it.

Another circular white shell is the **Lucina dentata** Wood. I have never found a perfect specimen, but single valves are occasionally cast up by the waves. The delicate sculpturing is peculiar and entirely different from any other species.

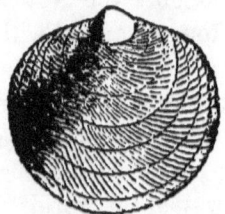

Fig. 22. Lucina dentata.

At Asbury Park and along the northern part of the coast, a very pretty dark chestnut brown species, **Astarte castanea** Say, is found.

Fig. 23. Astarte castanea.

It is a solid little clam of a peculiar and very graceful form, covered with a chestnut epidermis outside, white within. A number of related species are found upon the New England coast, but I have seen no Astarte but this one from New Jersey.

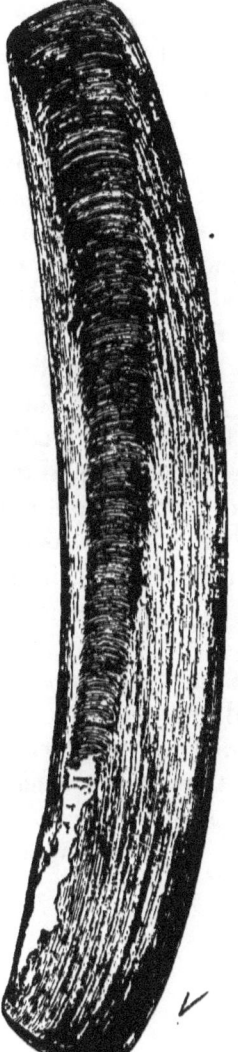

Fig. 25. Solen Americanus.

Tagelus gibbus Spengler, is a long clam, "gaping" or open at both ends. One valve has two long slender car-

Fig. 24. Tagelus gibbus.

dinal teeth, but in the other they are scarcely visible. When living in the sand they are covered with a yellow epidermis; but they usually live in mud, and are then almost free from this covering and stained black. The common size is nearly twice as large as this figure.

The curious family of Razor shells, *Solenidæ* have long, smooth shining shells, very beautiful when found alive or in good condition. They live in holes in the mud between tides, reaching their siphons to the surface when the water covers them. They dig with wonderful speed when danger, in the form of a shell-hunter or otherwise threatens, and about the only way to catch them alive is to cut off retreat by thrusting a spade under them.

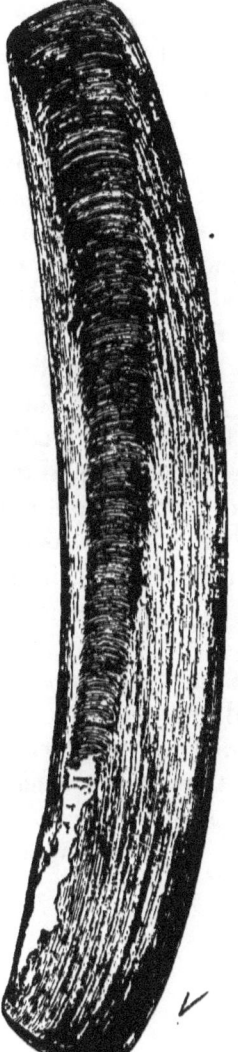

Fig. 25. Solen Americanus.

The largest is **Solen Americanus** Gould, the common American Razor Shell. The beaks are quite at the end of

of the shell, which is gently curved and from four to five inches long. It is very smooth, of an olive-brown color, somewhat stained with pink at the beaks and along a widening

Fig. 26. Siliqua costata.

band which extends forward from the beaks.

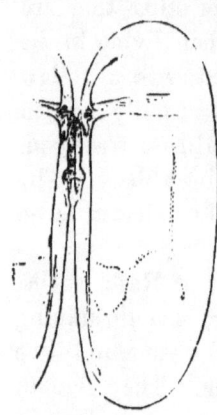

Very much like the American Razor Shell is the Green Razor Shell, **Solen viridis** Say; but this is much smaller than the other, rarely more than two inches long, and of a delicate green tint. The band extending from the beaks forward is not sharply defined as it is in the *Solen Americanus*. It is not frequently found.

Closely related to the Solens are the Ribbed Razors, **Siliqua costata** Say. The shell is oblong, rounded at both ends, the beaks at about a third of the length.

Fig. 27. Siliqua costata, inside.

Inside there is a strong white rib crossing from the beaks to the lower margin. The common length is from one to one and three-fourths inches.

CHAPTER V.—BORING BIVALVES.

The Piddocks (*Pholadidæ*) and the Ship Worms (*Teredidæ*) are more especially adapted for boring in wood, hard mud or stone than any other mollusks.

Fig. 29. Pholas truncata.

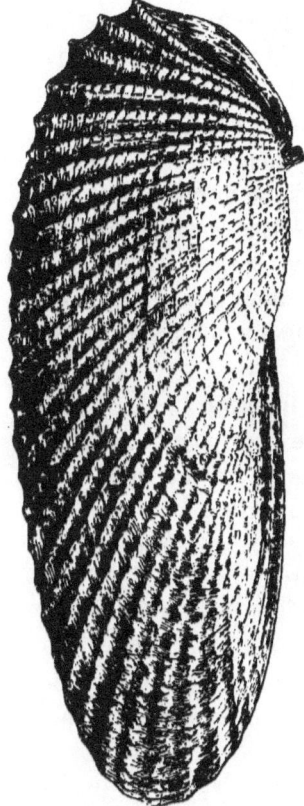

Fig 28. Pholas costata.

Fragments of the largest one of these, **Pholas costata** Linn., are frequently found on the beach after storms; but living specimens can only be had by dredging. Rarely perfect valves are thrown up. It is a most beautifully sculptured shell, pure white in color. The margin of the valves is turned outward over the beaks and there is a slender curved arm projecting from under the beaks.

25

A more abundant species is **Pholas truncata** Say. It bores in stiff mud, between tides, making a perpendicular round hole, sometimes a foot or more in depth. Fig. 29.

Zirphæa crispata Linn. is often found in soft wood. Its tunnels are very small at the opening, larger within. A whole colony sometimes lives in a single small piece of floating wood.

Fig. 30.   Zirphæa crispata.

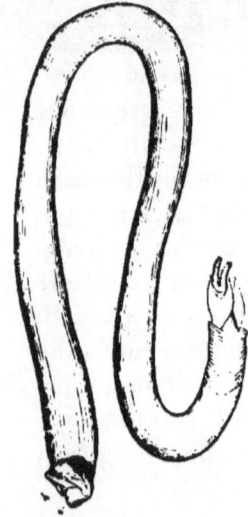

Fig. 31.   Teredo navalis.

The **Teredo navalis** Linn. or Ship Worm, is the pest of sea-faring men. It riddles wharfs or submarine woodwork of any kind, with its long tunnels, lined with a white chalky layer. The body of the Teredo is long and worm-like; the shell is small, and situated at the extreme end of the burrow. The shells are white and fragile, and have a certain resemblance to the *Pholas*.

Teredo, like other boring mollusks, does not eat the wood from its excavations, but obtains food from the sea water which it draws in through the perforation with which the burrow begins.

CHAPTER VI.—GASTEROPODS.

The univalve or *Gasteropod* mollusks are much more active and intelligent than the bivalves. They have a head, with eyes and tentacles or feelers. The mouth is at the end of a proboscis. The foot is flat and constructed for crawling. There is often a siphon to conduct water to the gills.

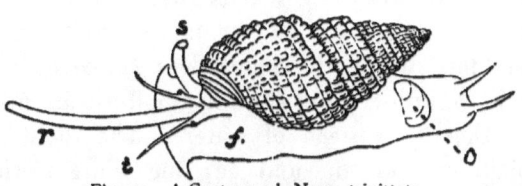

Fig. 32. A Gasteropod, Nassa trivittata.

The aperture of the shell is closed when the animal is retracted, by a small plate, the *operculum*.

The name *Gasteropod* means *stomach-foot*, in allusion to the fact that the entire lower surface of the body is thickened and flattened to form a broad muscular disk for crawling. This disk or "foot" is marked *f.* in the figure. Upon the back part of the foot, the operculum, *o*, is carried. The proboscis or *rostrum* is marked *r* in the figure. On each side of it, the tentacles, *t*, are situated, near the bases of which are the eyes. The tube marked *s* in the figure, conducts water to the gill cavity which is in the last whorl of the shell. When the animal retreats into the shell the water is squirted from the gill cavity to make room for the foot.

The Gasteropods may conveniently be divided into two classes, according to the shape of the aperture. In the herbivorous species the base of the aperture is rounded ; in the

27

carnivorous or flesh-eating species it has either a deep notch or is prolonged into a canal. This rule, however, is not without exceptions.

We will begin with **Melampus lineatus** Say, a small shell, not found on the open coast. It lives among the rank grass of the mudflats, where the water does not cover it; for Melampus, unlike all of the other mollusks in this book, breathes air instead of water. The shell is either plain or banded; and has fine white teeth within the aperture.

Melampus lineatus

The *Scalidæ*, Ladder shells, you will find on the beach. They have a long spire. The whorls are tubular, separated by deep sutures, and crossed by regular strong ribs. The aperture is oval.

None of the species are common on our coast; but the one most frequently met is **Scala Humphreysii** Kiener, a slender white species, having right rounded whorls. The riblets are rather widely separated, and upon each whorl there are eight or nine of them.

Scala Humphreysii.

Scala angulata Say is a stouter, shorter shell, rarely found.

Scala lineata Say has much more delicate riblets. It is brown, with a dark brown band near the base.

Bittium alternatum Say is a small slender shell, from one-fourth to five-sixteenths of an inch in length. The surface is cut into rounded beads by revolving and

Bittium alternatum.

longitudinal furrows. The color is light brown finely dotted with dark brown.

Another small slender shell is **Seila terebralis** Ad. It is of a more narrow and tapering form than Bittium, and has strong spiral ridges on the whorl. The aperture is deeply notched at its base.

Seila terebra-
lis.

CHAPTER VII.—HERBIVOROUS SNAILS.

A new-comer to our shores is the periwinkle, **Litorina litorea** Linn. Time was, and not many years ago, that this species was unknown south of Cape Cod. But during the last decade or two, the cry in the bivouacs of Litorina has been "southward ho!" And flourishing colonies at Point Pleasant, Atlantic City and other points, attest the success of their crusade. Our friends across the "pond" eat boiled periwinkles. Thousand of bushels annually are gathered for the London market.

Fig 37. Litorina litorea.

Another species of periwinkle, but this one a native American, comes from the Gulf up to mid-Jersey, and sometimes even further north. It is **Litorina irrorata** Say. It is narrower, more pointed than *L. litorea*, with a white mouth and orange-brown columella. It prefers salt grass to live in, and has an ambition to climb to the very top of the grass.

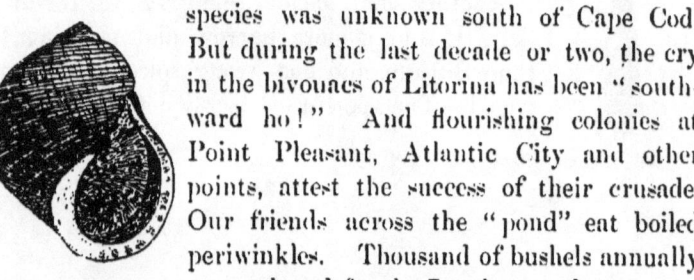

Fig. 38. Litorina irrorata.

Litorinella minuta.

Litorinella minuta Totten is the name of a tiny smooth shell somewhat related to the periwinkles. It has rounded whorls. It is of a light yellowish-gray tint, but when the animal is dried in it is blackish.

30

The family of Slipper Limpets or Boat Shells is one of the most numerous on our coast. These clumsy half-decked boats live wherever they find a shell, stone or bit of wood to cling to. The largest is **Crepidula fornicata** Linn. The curved beak (all that is left of what was a spire in its ancestors) is quite at the edge of the shell. The back is convex, white, speckled with reddish, and covered with a very thin yellowish epidermis. It is white inside, more or less clouded with purplish-brown. The white deck has a

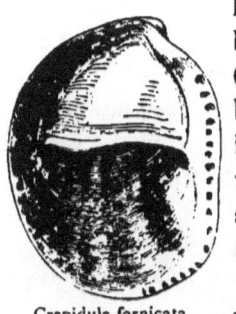

Crepidula fornicata.

wavy edge, and a decided notch on the left side. They live in all sorts of places; upon old Fulgur shells especially; and I have often seen individuals with a taste for travel on Horse-shoe crabs.

Living *inside* of all sorts and conditions of shells, often sharing these shelters with Hermit Crabs and its own brethren of the preceding species, we find the flat **Crepidula plana** Say. It is snowy-white, flat or concave outside, according to the curvature of its adopted home. The wonder is where such a flattened creature finds room for its organs

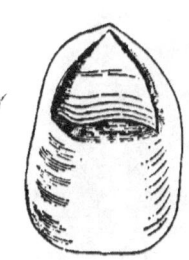

Crepidula plana.

at all. The deck is convex, its edge wavy, like that of *Crepidula fornicata*.

Another Boat Shell is found on our coast, **Crepidula convexa** ~~glauca~~ Say. This is smaller than *C. fornicata*. It is oval, convex, dark colored, about a half inch long. The apex forms a little hook a short distance away from the edge of the shell. The interior is dark brown, with a white deck. The edge of the deck is straighter than in the other two species, and it is not notched at the left end. When *C. glauca* grows on a flat

surface it is like this; but when it grows upon a small shell or pebble, it becomes very deep, very convex, the deck concave; but still the edge of the deck has the same form. This convex form of *C. glauca* is called variety *convexa* Say. They vary from dark to light or mottled in color.

Crepidula glauca, var.

C. glauca, var. convexa.

The *Naticidæ* or Moon Shell family have the appearance and organization of the plant-eating snails, but for all that, they have carnivorous habits. Their shells are globular, the aperture half-moon shaped, and closed by a thin plate or operculum. The fleshy part of the animal is very large. Naticidæ live

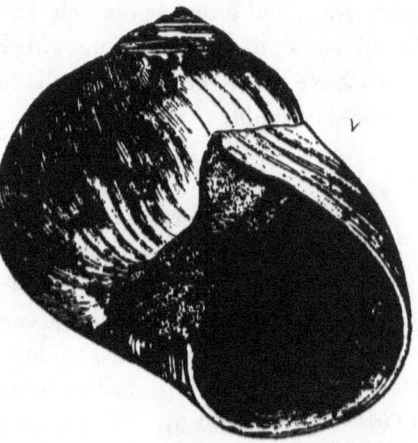

Fig. 44. Natica duplicata.

on sandy beaches, where they burrow along a little way below the surface, in search of bivalve mollusks upon which they feed. A peculiar little hillock, which one soon learns to recognize, shows where a Natica may be found under the sand.

Natica duplicata Say, the calloused moon-shell, is most abundant upon the sandy beaches of middle and southern New Jersey. It is large, brown or gray above but snowy white on the base around the tongue-shaped, rich chestnut brown callus which passes out of the aperture. This is a beautiful shell when perfect.

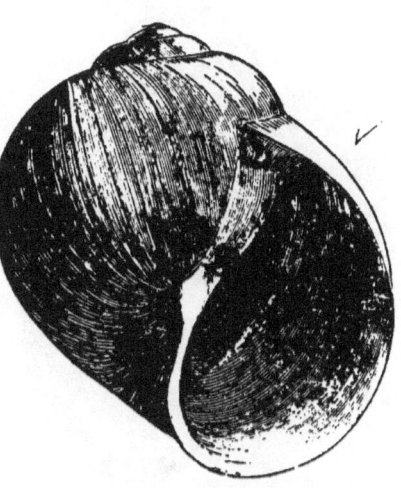

The Hero Natica, **Natica heros** Say, g r o w s e v e n larger than *N. duplicata,* but it has no callus, being open b e n e a t h. I have found it less abundant on this shore than the other species. There is quite a pretty variety occasionally met with which has the plainess of its ground-color relieved by three rows of brown spots.

Fig. 45. Natica heros.

It is known as *N. heros* variety *triseriata* Say.

N. heros var. triseriata.

The eggs of Natica are connected into a broad ribbon by soft mucus, which becomes covered and filled with sand, and curves into a shape like a saucer without a bottom, and with a segment broken from its rim. By holding this up to the light the small eggs may be seen through it.

✓

Buccinum undatum Linn. is a large whelk not often to be collected on our coast, although common northward. The shell has broad low waves upon the upper part.

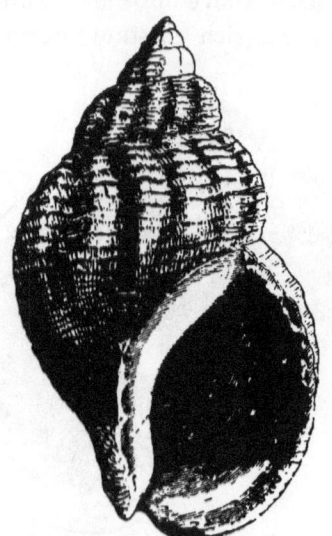

The banded whelk, **Nassa trivittata** Say, is not uncommon on sandy beaches. It is light colored with spiral brown bands. The surface is elaborately sculptured, being cut into beads arranged in close regular rows. It is often found containing the living animal.

Nassa vibex Say is stouter than the *N. trivittata*, with less distinct sculpture. It is not common in New Jersey.

Nassa trivittata.

Buccinum undatum.

Next to this clean looking species comes the Scavenger whelk, **Nassa obsoleta** Say. You will not find this black fellow living upon the clean fresh sands of the open shore; but go back to the mud flats and you see him in his element. His element, as I have said, is mud; and if it is

Nassa vibex.

Ilynassa oboleta Stimp (= Nassa obsoleta Say.)

34

sticky and black, and very deep, so much the better for him.

Nassa obso-
leta.

Fortunately, Nassas may be had without digging. Their crooked trails often cover the surface. And if one uses a tooth-brush vigorously upon them, the shells become really quite presentable.

The Fulgurs, or Conch Shells, are our largest gastropods. They are an exclusively American group, inhabiting the shores of the United States from Maine to Texas. We frequently see these

Fulgur canaliculata.

shells used as flowerbed borders and hanging baskets, together with the large pink-mouthed Conch, *Strombus gigas,* of the West Indies.

Fulgur canaliculata Say, the Velvet Conch, is pear-shaped and rather thin for so large a shell. The sutures of the spire are deeply channelled and a row of little tubercles surmounts the angle on the upper part. When fresh and perfect it

Fulgur carica.

Egg-cases of Fulgur carica.

is covered with a thin velvety epidermis of a buff color. The egg cases of this conch are often seen. They consist of a long string of capsules the shape of shallow saucers, held together by a tough cord attached to one edge of each. If the capsules are torn open, each is found to contain a number of young shells. The capsules of the Velvet conch have sharp edges, but those of *Fulgur carica* are angular and flat edged.

The Spiney conch, **Fulgur carica** Linn., is a much heavier, stronger shell than the preceding, and has no channel running along the suture, nor does it have a velvety epidermis. The angle of the whorls has short spines. The interior of the mouth is sometimes of a beautiful salmon color. The figure shows a short section from the string of egg-cases.

Urosalpinx cin- ereus.

The family *Muricidæ* contains a great many tropical shells very beautiful in color and contour, many of them being elaborately spined. Our cooler climate does not encourage exuberance in form or color, at least under water, although a different conclusion might be reached from an inspection of the fauna just above the water line. Our Muricidæ are very plain.

The common one is **Urosalpinx cinereus** Say, the "Drill" or oyster borer. The Drill is a typical carnivorous snail, and a deadly foe to the oyster-men. They destroy young oysters by boring through the shell, in the same way Natica attacks clams. The shell is fusiform ; largest in the middle, tapering toward both ends. They are sculptured with numerous spiral threads and rounded longitudinal folds.

Eupleura caudata.

An ally of the Drill, and a co-conspirator against the lives of tender young oysters, is **Eupleura caudata** Say.

This is a more angular species, with the outer lip strongly thickened. There is another thick rib or "varix" opposite the lip, giving the shell a flattened appearance. They grow nearly as large as Urosalpinx.

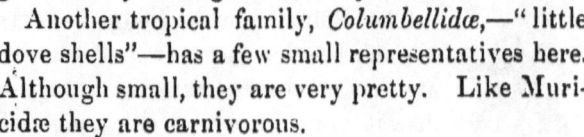

Another tropical family, *Columbellidæ,*—"little dove shells"—has a few small representatives here. Although small, they are very pretty. Like Muricidæ they are carnivorous.

Columbella lunata

Columbella lunata Say is small, smooth, marked with two series of new-moon shaped chestnut brown lines.

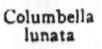

Columbella avara Say, is larger, with rather slender pointed spire. The base of the shell has spiral lines only; but above there are beautiful regular folds.

Columbella avara.

GLOSSARY.

ADDUCTOR MUSCLES. The muscles which connect the valves and pull them together.

APERTURE. The opening in a spiral shell.

APEX. The tip of the spire.

BEAKS. The first formed part of a bivalve shell. See figure 2. Also called the *Umbo*.

BIVALVE. A shell composed of two parts or valves, such as the Oyster and Clam.

CANAL. A narrow prolongation of the aperture of a spiral shell, for the protection of the siphon conducting water to its gills.

COLUMELLA. The pillar around which the whorls or turns of a spiral shell revolve.

EPIDERMIS. The horny coating which covers the outside of some shells.

LUNULE. A heart-shaped impressed area just below the beaks. It is prominent in the round clam, or *Venus*.

MANTLE. The fleshy or membranous lining of the shell.

OPERCULUM. A horny or shelly plate closing the aperture of a spiral shell.

PALLIAL LINE. The impressed line in the interior of a bivalve shell, where the mantle is attached. See figure 1.

PALLIAL SINUS. The bay or indentation in the pallial line, where the muscles which retract the siphons are attached. See figure 1. Clams with short siphons have no pallial sinus.

SIPHONS. The tubes through which water is drawn to the gills and mouth of a bivalve, and expelled from them when used.

SPIRE. All of the whorls of a spiral shell except the last one, together form the spire.

SUTURE. The line where the turns of a spiral shell unite.

TEETH. The tooth-like projections upon the hinge of a bivalve shell.

UMBILICUS. The cavity in the base of a shell in which the columella or axis is hollow; such as *Natica heros.*

UMBO. See figure 2. Also called *beaks.*

UNIVALVE. A shell composed of one part only, such as the Conch.

VALVE. One of the two parts of a bivalve shell, such as a clam.

WHORLS. The spiral turns of a shell.

www.ingramcontent.com/pod-product-compliance
Lightning Source LLC
Chambersburg PA
CBHW030914260626
47169CB00008B/2844